Island in the Sky

Publication Date: September 10, 2018

AQUARIOTS
U N L I M I T E D

ISBN-13: 978-1-7750252-6-9

The Ramseys walked along the sunlit path that led through the uncultivated fields to town. Mr. Ramsey, a tall fellow with a wiry frame despite all his years felling trees, held one of the mule's reins as he kept pace alongside it with his wife. The simple lorry the mule pulled had no driver's bench, only a flat cartbed to carry all the long planks of

1

lumber to be sold at the market.

Mrs. Ramsey thought she heard a faint giggling despite the trundle of the wheels. She turned her head toward the meadow on the right, where it had seemed to come from. "Did you hear that?" she asked her husband, who blankly followed her gaze. The sound came more distinctly this time, and she put a hand in front of Mr. Ramsey's chest. "Shh!" He obligingly brought the rumbling cart to a stop, and they listened for a moment. Into the silence rose another bout of baby-like laughter and cooing. "It sounds like a child," she breathed, and headed off in the direction of it. Hesitating, Mr. Ramsey looked around, then led the mule over to a shrubby tree and tied the reins to a branch before trailing after his wife.

Mrs. Ramsey drew up short at what she saw. A blonde girl, little more than a year old, sat amidst the tall grass, giggling in delight as she batted at the stalks with her little hand. She wore a pretty sky-blue dress with gathered capsleeves. A yellow-and-black butterfly fluttered past her face, and her eyes latched onto it. She cooed, reaching out for it.

Mrs. Ramsey stared at her in bewilderment. "How did you get all the way out here?" She looked out over the landscape, scanning all around for where the girl's family might be, but there was no one in sight. What kind of people would leave a toddler in the middle of nowhere? *And how long has it been since she ate*? Mrs. Ramsey stooped and lifted the girl up into her arms.

"Don't go jus' pickin' up a strange child," Mr. Ramsey protested.

"We can't just leave her here," she countered. It was her natural motherly instinct to get the wee thing off the ground and keep her safe. Besides, the tot didn't seem to mind; she looked perfectly content, simply putting her knuckles in her mouth. Mrs. Ramsey noticed the sparkle of a silver necklace at the babe's neck, and lifted its fine chain, on which hung a set of carved letters that spelled out a name. "Celeste," she read. She didn't know of anybody around here who could afford such pricy jewelry for their children. She hadn't seen anyone with quite so bonnie a baby, either. "Let's see if anyone in town is missing her."

They returned to the path and continued on for another hour until they reached the village. On their way to the market, they asked everyone they saw if Celeste was theirs or if they knew of anyone who had lost track of their toddler, but all they got were shaken heads and quizzical looks. While Mr. Ramsey bartered with the timber merchant, Mrs. Ramsey kept asking around nearby. She also bought Celeste a soft cookie treat, to make sure she didn't go hungry. Once the sale of the wood was made, they even went around knocking on doors, though the few who did answer often found the intrusion irritating or were indignant at the accusation that they'd misplace their own child. Finally, the Ramseys drifted back into the square, with no choice but to conclude that Celeste's family wasn't in this town. But the next closest settlements were miles away, too far for a tot to have wandered from. And the Ramseys couldn't go and check them all. Hopefully word of their little search would spread to whomever she did belong to, whether it was someone they missed here or elsewhere.

Mrs. Ramsey sighed. "Well, looks like no one here will claim the poor thing." She looked down at Celeste with indecision. "Maybe...we should keep her."

Mr. Ramsey's straggly eyebrows went up. "We can't afford another mouth to feed.

We've a hard enough time keeping ourselves fed."

"We've been putting some money away."

"That's fer retirement! I won't be able to keep choppin' wood ferever! Besides, we're too old to be raisin' another youngun from scratch."

"Oh, nonsense. I'm not yet fifty, and you don't have many years on me. We can handle a little darling like her." She touched a tender finger onto the tip of the girl's nose. "I always wanted a daughter."

"What use have we for a girl? She won't be cut out fer labour like sons are."

"We already had four of those. Good-for-nothin's. They all off workin' their own crafts and farms, with never a thought for how we're getting by."

"That's jus' 'cause lumberjackin' ain't a trade as can be passed on. They jus' tryin' to make more prosperous lives fer themselves."

"Well, knowin' them, they won't be wantin' another baby neither, not when they got more of their own on the way. We're all this child has."

"I still say it's none of our business," Mr. Ramsey muttered. He watched Celeste for a quiet moment as she sucked on her necklace, looking up at them with big green eyes. "She is a precious t'ing, though," he murmured, and stroked a gentle hand on her blonde head. Then he set a fist on his hip and scowled. "Awright, we'll take her in," he declared grudgingly, and Mrs. Ramsey beamed. "But she's goin' back at the first sign of her parents comin' to get her!"

"Absolutely!" Hiking the tot closer, Mrs. Ramsey started off for home, her grumbling husband trailing behind with the mule cart.

~ *Chapter 1* ~

Celeste gazed up at the distant island, suspended high in the blue sky. She often came here to look at it. And to wonder what it was like up there. She'd heard tales of it ever since she was a little girl, even in the far southwest, and it had always fascinated her. A few globular white clouds floated near the horizon and around the isle, not much higher than it. A gull coasted along through the air, then landed on the grassy brink of the island. It was so odd that they had a perch higher than any tree rising from the ground. It wasn't a very large parcel of land, but it was still visible for miles around. Tourists came from all over to visit the single most extraordinary phenomenon in the world. In fact, Celeste caught a glint of sunlight off a shuttlecraft that was slowly heading there now, to convey its load of passengers. But her family had never been able to afford the fare.

The tall grasses around her swayed in the breeze, brushing against the skirt of her light-blue dress. She absently stroked her hand over their tips. A stronger gust tossed her wavy blonde hair about, and she sighed, pushing it back with her hands. *I'd better get back home.* She turned to walk back through the bright yellow-green field.

It was a long way back to the house,

and by the time she got there, the island was little more than a faraway dot behind her. Green fields of rye surrounded the modest farmhouse of faded wooden boards. One of Mrs. Ramsey's sons had let his mother and Celeste stay here in an extra building on the far side of his farm. They'd moved here five years ago, after Mr. Ramsey passed. Celeste still missed him and his simple gentleness sometimes. In his later years, when he was too old to keep logging, he'd taken up carving, which had always been a hobby. But there wasn't much of a market for whimsical owl sculptures, and it wasn't as lucrative as the timber trade even when there were buyers. Their funds had dwindled, and after he was gone, they'd had no source of income at all. There were always plenty of strong young men coming from town to cut down trees in the forest they lived near, and they weren't about to share any of the profits with the Ramsey women. They couldn't afford to keep living there, so they'd had no choice but to leave the house and stay with one of Mrs. Ramsey's sons in the area. But each of them had their hands full with their own teeming families and demanding work, and didn't have spare room or money to accommodate them for long. Then, finally, they'd gotten a letter back from her farmer son in the midland, who was slightly more well-off and had a spare house available for them. Celeste still thought of him as Mrs. Ramsey's son, not really her own brother, though she'd always called the Ramseys Mother and Father.

She'd known from the beginning that she was a foundling. But where she came from was an unsolvable mystery; all the Ramseys knew was that her name was Celeste, from her necklace. She was grateful that they hadn't kept the knowledge from her, but as a result, she'd always felt a bit distanced from her family, different than the other children who were raised by their birth parents. It didn't help that the Ramsey boys hadn't spent much time with her when they did visit, and the one they were living with now hadn't even met her before she got there.

When Celeste stepped in the door, she heard talking in the kitchen ahead.

"You know I'm fine with boarding you here, but that Celeste is another matter." It was the voice of Mrs. Ramsey's son. "The least she could do is help you out around the house more. But she's too dignified for that, of course."

Celeste drifted across the dim sitting room toward the archway.

"She does help. She keeps me company when no one else does." Mrs. Ramsey's tone was rather pointed.

"Where is she now, then? She's always off staring at that island, wasting time with

13

her head up in the clouds. She's a grown woman – she should be married by now, or at least looking for a husband among the many young men in the towns around here. Then she'd be his responsibility."

Celeste came near enough to see into the other room. Mrs. Ramsey, a stocky but weathered woman, stood on the other side of the kitchen table facing her son. Her grey hair, streaked with a few white strands, was rolled at the nape of her neck as usual. She squared her shoulders in response to her son's comment. "She'll get married when she's good an' ready! If it's not somethin' she wants to do yet, I ain't gonna force her to!"

Her eyes flicked to Celeste as she came in, and Farmer Ramsey turned his head to glance at Celeste too. He was in his forties, and his own children were nearly Celeste's age, so it was little wonder he couldn't quite see her as a sister.

"Don't argue on account of me," Celeste said quietly. She never wanted there to be conflict. She'd even mediated little disagreements between Mr. and Mrs. Ramsey when she was younger. It was harder to do when she was the subject of the dispute.

Farmer Ramsey brushed past Celeste on his way out. "See you later."

Celeste continued closer to Mrs. Ramsey. "Maybe I *should* think of something to profit the family."

Mrs. Ramsey gave her a slight smile. "Don't let him get to you. He's just worried about the income from his crops this year."

Celeste sighed. "I wish Father was here."

Mrs. Ramsey wrapped a comforting arm around her shoulders. "I know. As do I."

~ *Chapter 2* ~

Celeste came downstairs the next morning and went into the sunlit kitchen to prepare some breakfast for herself and Mrs. Ramsey. She heard the front door creak open and closed, and then Mrs. Ramsey came shuffling in, looking through a handful of letters.

Her steps halted abruptly. "Oh,

Celeste, look what came in the mail for you today! It says you've won a trip to the Floating Island!" She handed Celeste a shimmering golden ticket.

Her heart leapt as she took it. "What? But I haven't entered a lottery..." She looked down at it.

CELESTE RAMSEY,
    YOU'VE BEEN RANDOMLY SELECTED
        AS 1 OF 100 LUCKY WINNERS OF
    A FREE DAY TRIP TO THE FLOATING ISLAND!

PRESENT THIS TICKET AT THE SHUTTLE STATION
WITHIN THE NEXT 2 WEEKS AND ENJOY YOUR VISIT!

She could hardly believe it. She glanced up. "May I, Mother?"

"Of course! I know how much you've always wanted to go."

"But I'll still have to get there

somehow..." It would be too far to walk.

Mrs. Ramsey thought for a minute. Then she lifted a finger. "Oh! I think one of the neighbouring farmers is going to be cartin' another batch of supplies to the island – in just a few days' time, if I'm not mistaken. I'm sure he wouldn't mind giving you a lift."

"But he won't be staying there for hours, will he? How will I get back?"

Mrs. Ramsey paused. "Maybe you can hitch a ride back with some other tourists headed this way. I'll give you a few of my spare coins in case you need to pay fer transport for yourself. If nothin' else, I'll borrow my son's draft horse and come get you myself."

Celeste smiled in appreciation. She was grateful that at least Mrs. Ramsey still had her back.

"I'll go check with the neighbour this afternoon," Mrs. Ramsey added.

Celeste could hardly contain her expectancy for the few hours until Mrs. Ramsey set out to the adjacent farm, and had an even harder time waiting for her to get back. When she finally returned, it was all Celeste could do to keep from bobbing on her toes as Mrs. Ramsey hung up her shawl on the wall peg beside the front door before she began speaking.

"Don't look so anxious, Celeste! The farmer says it's fine."

Celeste clasped her hands in delight.

"It's three days from now. But he'll be headin' out at first light, so you'll have to be ready by then."

That was fine by Celeste; it just meant all the more hours of daylight she could spend on the island.

Celeste got up at dawn on the designated day, and put on her best dress – a simple, draping, floor-length gown of dusky grey, with a soft collar and long, slightly flared sleeves. She slid her golden ticket into a flat pocket sewn onto the hip of the skirt, along with the five coppers Mrs. Ramsey had given her. She didn't pack anything else, since she would be back home in time for supper.

She gave Mrs. Ramsey a goodbye kiss on the cheek on her way out and hastened through the dim fields to meet the neighbour at his farm. She climbed up onto the cartbench beside the wizened old man, who then flapped the reins to start his weary nag plodding.

After a while of silence, the farmer made an attempt at conversation. "So, I hear you won a tour of the island. That's some trip."

Celeste turned to him avidly. "Have you ever been?"

"Oh, gracious, no. I'm not terribly

21

fond of heights. I don't see what all the fuss is about, livin' on a chunk of land way up in the air, all precarious-like. I much prefer the good ol' solid ground, meself."

Celeste looked away, suppressing a bit of a smile. He reminded her a little of Mr. Ramsey. He'd always been the down-to-earth sort, too.

She lifted her eyes to the faraway island, and watched it slowly grow closer as the hours dragged on.

***

The captain stood with fists on his hips, watching his men heft the canister down from the covered wagon onto the ground before him. He ran his hand down the smooth steel. The cylinder stood as high as a man, with many airtight seams and interlocking mechanisms, as well as a smaller, sealed pipe rising from the top. He'd found it deep within a cave while looting the stash of another pirate. Legend said it would unleash a terrible power that could take control of others. And the captain reckoned that if he was the one to release it, command of that power would be his, like letting a djinn out of a bottle.

But it could only be opened at an altitude higher than seven thousand feet. Even if there were a mountain nearby, it would be too laborious to climb it and lug the canister along with them. He only knew of one place that was that far up. He turned to look out from the small stand of trees they stood in, at the sky-island in the distance. The Floating Land.

He lowered his eyes to the shuttle station below it. All they would have to do was wait for one of the shuttles to empty of tourists, then slip aboard behind cover of the crowd and fly it to the island after picking up the canister from the copse. It should be doable without attracting attention. But if someone *did* get in their way... The captain pushed back his long red coat to rest his hand on the wood handle of his iron pistol, and smirked. He'd have to do some convincing.

~ *Chapter 3* ~

The farmer pulled his cart up. "This is my stop," he told Celeste. She thanked him for the lift and stepped down off the side of the wagon bench. The island loomed high in the sky overhead. She'd never been this close to it. The shuttle station was still well outside its shadow, which lay some distance further ahead.

A large crowd milled around the station. As Celeste became caught up in the eddying tide of people, an official directed her and the others with an arm held out. "Incomers this way. Single file."

The tourists ahead of her formed a line, and soon Celeste could see they were being herded down a lane that led beside a small ticket booth. There were several more in a row to either side. Beyond this one, a shuttle rested atop four thick supports standing several feet high, a section of its side lowered to make a ramp reaching the ground. The shuttle was made of silvery-grey metal panels, with a slanted, tinted windshield wrapping partway around, and a high window across the length of each side.

As they came up, the previous batch of tourists were disembarking from another shuttle on the left. Celeste arrived in time to see the last one lift a necklace off over his head, depositing it in the small opening of a varnished wooden box on the counter.

The person ahead of her finished paying the fellow manning the admissions booth, and the rest of the queue proceeded closer to the waiting shuttle.

When Celeste got to the booth, she brought out her golden ticket for the man to see, and he nodded, letting her keep it. But before she got on the shuttle, she had to sign a waiver providing her first and last name and next of kin, releasing the inhabitants of the Floating Land from liability in the event of the undersigned suffering from altitude sickness, falling off the edge of the island, or any number of other unfortunate eventualities. Celeste felt a bit of trepidation, but swallowed and signed the paper. She'd come too far to turn back now. Besides, things like that hardly ever happened anyway; they just had to list all the remote possibilities to cover their bases.

Then it was her turn to approach the shuttle and walk up the entry ramp into it.

The interior was big enough for about twenty people, with a row of upholstered grey benches on either side of a wide aisle. Celeste went to take an unoccupied seat on the right. Once the rest of the places had been filled by tourists, the hatch slowly lifted and closed. It was quieter and dimmer inside now, and strips of white crystal glowed along the floor to mark the sides of the aisle.

A female attendant stepped out of a door at the front of the shuttle, where a compartment was sectioned off for the pilot. "Please remain seated for the duration of the ride," she said to the passengers in a cool voice. "Liftoff will now commence. We will arrive at the island in a few minutes." Then she went back in.

The shuttle started sluggishly, lifting

off the struts and turning to ascend gradually toward the island. Celeste felt a sort of giddy suspense in her middle. She looked out the window beside her, watching the ground shrink away, until the haze of an interposing cloud obscured it from view. Then she craned her neck to look forward out of the glass.

A few wisps of cloud passed over the shuttle's nose, and then they broke out into a spectacular panorama. They were amidst a field of clouds, slowly rising between towering masses of bright white domes with shadowed underbellies. They were even more beautiful and immense from here. It took her breath away to be above the clouds.

For as long as she could remember, she'd always had dreams of clouds. This was almost like that – except, of course, in the dream, she'd been gliding among them without a shuttle.

The attendant came out again and

paced down the aisle between the seats. "We are now approaching five thousand feet."

Celeste watched the shadow of their shuttle pass over the white clouds beside them. She spotted another ahead of it, and looked out the window on the left side, to see another shuttleship go past them, heading down to the mainland.

Another minute passed, and they emerged into a greater expanse of blue sky.

"We are nearing our destination at eight thousand feet."

The shuttle started turning to get into position for landing, until Celeste could see the island. Beneath its flat top side, a large mass of solid dirt, roots and even vines tapered down.

The shuttle came low over the isle and slowed to a stop, hovering in place. Then its hatch hissed and opened outward and down to rest on the ground, letting in the sunlight.

"You may now exit in an orderly fashion," the attendant prompted. "You are now guests of the Floating Land."

Momentous anticipation rose in Celeste as she got up from her seat and followed the other passengers down the ramp. She tried to get a look past their heads at the view beyond.

"Please stay away from the edge of the island," a resonant voice called out from somewhere on the right. Several guides stood around the perimeter, a few paces in from the brink, with their arms spread. Their trim pale-blue uniforms were slashed with silver strips that reflected in the daylight. One was speaking into a crystal that somehow amplified his voice. "Make sure you have a levitation pendant to keep you from falling."

A representative waiting at the end of the downramp lowered a necklace around the head of each tourist in the line as they

31

passed. When it was Celeste's turn, she was given one too. She held it up in her hand and looked at it as she followed the crowd drifting farther inland. On a simple black string hung a white glass marble with blue swirls. It must've been what she saw the one tourist put in the box. They must have to return the necklaces once they reached the mainland again. It was too bad; it would've made a good souvenir.

Celeste lifted her head and took her first good look at the Floating Land. It was a level expanse of lush grass in a roughly circular shape, about fifty yards across, with a wide, resplendent mansion in the middle and a few leafy trees on either side. She wondered if the trees could tell they were aloft in the middle of the sky.

She looked up at the sky – or the upper half of it – basking in the glow. Was she actually closer to the sun? She turned to peer past the edge of the island, down at the fields so far below. The trees and homesteads were nothing but specks, the farmland mere strips of different greens, and the shadows of clouds – as well as some of the lower clouds themselves – were small patches that passed lazily over the ground. She could see so far in all directions, until everything became hazed with blue in the distance. She would've thought she'd find it dizzying – as some of the others clearly did – but instead it was exhilarating.

Celeste turned back to survey the isle. A small puffy cloud floated on the left, at about the same height as the island. The breeze brought it in, and it hovered a few inches from the ground, drifting along over the grass. A little boy ran giggling over to it, and put a hand out over its round top as if to pet it, though his hand would only pass through it.

"If you'll all follow me," the same announcer prompted, "I will be giving a tour of the grounds, before you go inside." Celeste looked around to see that the last of the other tourists had left the shuttle. She joined them as they gravitated into a straggly group behind the guide, who headed to the northeast.

A cumulus cloud approached from the side, larger than the whole island. It drew closer, enshrouding the west half of the isle, and soon they were completely enveloped in a white haze. Cool moisture surrounded her, omnipresent in the air. Celeste looked around in awe. She lifted a hand, and fine water droplets collected on it. She could hardly believe she was *inside* a cloud. It brought back all her childlike wonder, made her feel more like herself than she had in a long time.

There were mutters from the other tourists as they lost sight of everything that was more than a few feet away.

"There is no cause for concern," the guide reassured. "The cloud is entirely harmless, but it will cause low visibility. Please remain in place until the cloud has passed."

A minute later, the fog began to move off to the right, revealing the sunlit lawn again – now sprinkled with dew. Celeste turned her head to watch the cloud scud off the other side of the island, for the most part intact. It must be so surreal to live in a place that the clouds passed right through.

The guide resumed leading the way to the right of the mansion, until they arrived at a small round pond about twenty feet across. Celeste leaned over to peer in at the bottom, wondering how far down it went. Only a few feet; the island itself wasn't very deep. Somehow she hadn't thought there would be a pocket of water on the sky island. Its clear waters allowed sight of several clusters of raw blueish crystals that peeked out from the sides around the inner circumference. Dappled shade danced across half the surface, cast by a nearby elm. "This pond supplies the mansion with drinking water, without relying solely on the barrels that are brought here on shuttles, as our food is. The crystals lining its interior keep it pristine. It is refilled when it rains."

It hadn't occurred to her that it must rain here too. And it would reach this place sooner than the ground below. But then where would it go? It must drain off the edge of the island...and then it would still be dripping onto the land beneath even after the rain had stopped elsewhere. She wouldn't want to live directly under it, especially since it would be draped in noon shadow every day. But if the rainclouds were at a lower altitude than the island...it would still be sunny with clear blue skies up here, even while it was pouring on the rest of the land. It was so peculiar to envision.

The guide showed them around the back of the mansion, where there was a wide patio of large, flat, square stones, then kept onward around the other side of the house. Just before they rounded the corner, Celeste glanced over her shoulder and noticed the top of a shuttle creeping up into sight from below the island's edge. Strange; Celeste thought they only landed at the front to unload and load passengers. That was the direction they came from, after all.

Once the guide brought them back around to the front again, Celeste studied the place while she and the other people approached its open entrance. It was made of blocks of white stone that shone in the sunlight, topped with a gently sloping roof tiled in midnight-blue slate. The front windows on the ground floor were wide, and the main structure had a one-storey wing on each side. Vines with dark green leaves climbed the corners of the building and also coiled around the columns that stood on either side of the front door to support an overhang. The leaves fluttered as Celeste passed between them and stepped inside.

~ *Chapter 4* ~

Princess Raianna sighed, looking out the mansion's front window at the milling tourists. "Must we keep holding these monthly ticket giveaways? It grows so tiresome doing this same thing over and over."

"It's our best chance of finding the White Princess," the counsellor reminded placidly, coming up beside her with his arms folded.

She turned to him, spreading her hands. "It's been twenty years! Don't you think if my sister was going to visit the island, she would have by now?"

"We've only been hosting the lottery for seven. There are thousands of Celestes in the world. But we *are* narrowing down those left to invite."

"Who's to say she even goes by that name anymore? If she was taken in by someone, they could have named her anything."

"She *was* wearing her necklace when she went missing. We have to hope she didn't lose it. Even if she did, then she's just as likely to be any of the other tourists."

Raianna started pacing over the granite floor of the drawing room, the long skirt of her red dress swishing. "I wish we had a way of knowing more about them first. Last time, there was a Celeste who was sixty-three years old, and another who was only seven."

"At least it's easy to rule them out on sight." The counsellor resumed peering out the glass. "I only saw a few blonde women step off the shuttles today. It shouldn't take me long to follow up on each of them."

"How can we be sure it's her even if she does come? What if she's already been here and gone and we didn't know it?"

The counsellor gave her a slight smile of fond amusement. "Have a little faith, Princess. We will know. If nothing else, the island itself will recognize her."

He headed out through the archway, and Raianna allowed his words to reassure her. The counsellor was almost like a father to her, when she barely remembered her parents. He'd managed the kingdom while she was a minor, had been her invaluable advisor ever since she'd ascended to the throne at just thirteen. He reminded her to be more optimistic sometimes – but she was the pragmatic one; it had always been in her nature to be skeptical. It had never been her who was meant to rule. Not for the first time, Raianna wished for the day her sister would come and lift the onus of leadership from her.

***

As Celeste and the others entered the mansion, a middle-aged man in slate-blue attire came into the hall from an archway on the right. He stopped before them with his hands clasped behind his back, and smiled. "Welcome, everyone! I am the counsellor to the current ruler of The Island in the Air. I will be guiding you on a tour of the mansion today. Please remain in a group and refrain from touching anything."

He held out an arm and started off through an arch on their left, while Celeste and the tourists trailed behind him in a cluster.

"Here's the sitting room," the counsellor began. The dark floorboards were polished to a soft sheen, and several landscape paintings hung on the papered walls above carved wainscoting. A sculpted wooden settee with red upholstery ran the length of the wall on the right, and there were even a few gold or jade vases on marble pedestals in the corners. Celeste had never seen such elegant furnishings, though they didn't exceed practicality.

A servant came out of a door opposite them and gave them a nod in passing.

The counsellor went on, "The retainers of the royal house also live here in the mansion, in several of the dozen rooms on the second floor. Most are native-born islanders, the sole citizens of the Floating Land, whose families have served as loyal subjects for generations. Some of them take on the duties of guides during these tourist events."

The group lingered and looked around at the decor for a minute, with a few admiring mutters.

"On to the dining room." When they headed out the other archway in the far corner, the counsellor gestured to a parted door in the same wall beside them. "That leads down to the cellar, within the very heart of the island."

Ahead, in a nook formed by a dividing wall, the back door stood open a crack. Its inset window, with the sash lifted an inch to let in a fresh breeze, overlooked the patio. In the north wall, two large windows let in plenty of light onto a long, darkwood dining table lined with chairs.

The counsellor crossed the room and proceeded down another hallway, to an arch on the left. They toured the kitchen – where a few cooks were starting to prepare lunch, and which had an adjoining pantry for storing the provisions brought by the shuttles – and the archive library, through a door at the end of the corridor, where matters of state were discussed.

Then the counsellor led them into a spacious room made entirely of white marble. "And this is the throne room, otherwise known as The Hall of the Rising Sun." The whole eastern wall was covered in ceiling-high windows that looked out on a clear view over the edge of the island. Celeste imagined how the people here would have to watch the sun rise from below them, and it would take several hours before its rays even reached the top side of the island. It must be so otherworldly. In the center of the floor was a raised circular dais. "Royal announcements and coronations are made here, while standing on the dais facing east, in the direction of new beginnings."

They continued into the drawing room, with floors of granite, and then ended up back in the same entry hall they'd started in.

Through the arch to the sitting room, Celeste saw a brunette woman in a stately, dark-red dress. She stood with her back to Celeste amidst a gaggle of curious tourists.

"Thank you all for coming!" the counsellor concluded to the group Celeste was in. "You may resume exploring the island. A shuttle should be arriving shortly with another load of tourists from the mainland. You can take it back down once they disembark."

Most of the people started filtering

out the open front door. But Celeste lingered, a little disappointed as she looked around. She didn't want to leave already. After so many years of wishing, it didn't seem sufficient to just visit the island for barely an hour. Besides, her ticket was for a 'day trip'. Maybe she could just take a later shuttle back.

The counsellor came up to her. "Good day. Are you by chance the recipient of one of the golden tickets for a free trip?"

"Oh – yes," she replied, fishing the ticket out of her pocket to show him.

He leaned a bit closer to inspect the name on it. "Then you're eligible for an exclusive tour of the royal portrait gallery!" He turned aside and gestured with a hand.

Celeste was delighted. It was just the kind of thing she'd been hoping for. Maybe it was a little overgenerous, when she'd already gotten a free pass here in the first place, but she wasn't about to turn down the chance to stay longer and see a special room.

The counsellor went to open a door up the hall on the right, and they entered a long, narrow gallery with gold-inlaid floors. Dozens of large paintings in gilded frames hung side-by-side along the length of the left-hand wall. "The Silverborn family has ruled this island for as long as it has been in the sky," the counsellor began as they paced down the row of portraits of past kings and queens.

Near the end, they stopped in front of one depicting a regal couple sitting together. The brunette woman held a blonde baby girl in a white dress, perched on her knee. The man had fair hair sweeping halfway to his shoulders, and a beard only around his mouth. There was a gentle wisdom in his eyes.

"These were the last rulers of the

Floating Land," the counsellor said with a trace of sadness in his voice. "They both perished of fever when their second daughter was only seven years old. It was a great loss for us all."

"Is that her?" Celeste prompted, indicating the baby in the picture.

"No, this is their firstborn, the White Princess."

Celeste paused, studying the girl's green eyes. They looked somehow familiar.

"She was always destined to be the one true ruler of the Floating Land, for she possessed the wise and just nature needed in a Preserver of Peace. But, nineteen years ago, she went missing from the island, when she was little more than a year old."

Celeste looked at the counsellor in commiserative dismay.

"We searched the whole mansion and grounds, and began to worry that she'd fallen off. She did wear her levitation pendant at all times, so she'd be safe, but she could still be suspended in the air anywhere around or below the island.

"Then we noticed several of our expensive items were gone as well. A shuttle had recently departed after delivering a shipment of supplies, and we realized the only ones who could have done it were the delivery men." As an aside, the counsellor added, "Back then, it wasn't uncommon for the freighter to be our only visitor in the whole month. After that, we had the unloaders just leave the crates on the lawn, and only let our own trusted retainers bring them inside the mansion." Then he turned back to regard the portrait. "We feared the thieves had taken the Princess too, and planned to hold her for ransom. We sent out shuttles in every direction to try to catch them, but by then they were long gone. They hadn't landed the shuttle on the mainland anywhere near here, so they must have driven it back to their hideout. We scoured the land for miles around, asking everyone if they'd seen a blonde tot matching the White Princess' description, or any suspicious sellers of stolen merchandise, for that matter.

"Time went on, but a ransom demand never came. We wondered if perhaps the Princess had accidentally stowed away on board their shuttle and they didn't know it. If that was the case, we hoped they'd let her go once they discovered her. But we found no trace of her in the area. We persisted for weeks, but we only have so many people that could be sent out, and our jurisdiction only extends so far. We couldn't cover the whole world. So, dejected, we returned to our island, knowing she must be in one of the distant places we hadn't gotten to yet."

Celeste had listened enrapt to it all.

She'd never heard word of this back in the southwest.

"Without her, the island is slowly deteriorating, which it never has before. We used to be at a height of ten thousand feet. Now it is sinking lower by a hundred feet each year."

Celeste's heart lurched. *Oh no.*

"The island was once larger as well, but its edges have been crumbling, a little every week. In less than eighty years, the Floating Land will be nothing more than a pile of earth on the ground – if there's anything left of it at all."

She put a hand over her chest. It would be a tragedy if such a marvel of nature were to be no more.

"But we retain the hope that the White Princess will return one day to take her rightful place on the throne, and restore our land to its proper balance." The counsellor looked right at her. "Her name is Celeste."

Her stomach leapt. "That's my name," she murmured.

He showed a rueful smile. "I know. In each batch of those free tickets we've been sending out, twenty of them are addressed to women named Celeste, in the hopes that one of them turns out to be our Princess."

"Oh." Celeste felt easier about it, if a little sheepish. Of course she wasn't the only one.

They moved on to the next painting. "And this one is Raianna, the red princess." It was an elegant young woman in a crimson dress, standing proud with her hands folded at her waist and her chin up. Her brunette hair cascaded down her shoulders, but there was something about her stern brown eyes and hard cheekbones that made her seem older than she must have been. "You may have seen her around the mansion. Only a year younger than Celeste, she's been the reigning princess since she was thirteen. She never knew her sister, but she's been waiting for her for nineteen years."

~ *Chapter 5* ~

Celeste and the counsellor came out of the gallery into the back room of the mansion. They stood for a moment in somber silence as Celeste thought about the stories of the Silverborns. Then she lifted her head, catching the faintest whiff.

"Does something on the air smell odd to you?" she asked the counsellor in a murmur, drifting to the slightly ajar back door to investigate. When she stopped just back from it, a whisper of wind came through the gap under the partially lifted window-pane. There was definitely a cold metallic scent on the breeze, with an almost sickly element to it that seemed much more sinister.

On the patio ahead, there were two fellows tinkering with a large steel canister. Celeste had a very unsafe feeling. She closed and locked the door, just for caution's sake. Beyond the men, a shuttle with an open hatch waited near the edge of the island. Then she saw a vague shimmering in the air to the right, a wavering zigzag line almost of cloud, but it was gone again in a trice. She slid the window down for good measure, ensuring it was shut tight. Whatever it was, it was clearly airborne.

The men noticed it, too, and appeared to be spurred into fear by it; when the shuttle veered and made a getaway, they came rushing up to the door and tried to get inside, but the handle wouldn't move.

"Let us in!" they shouted desperately through the glass, banging on it with their fists. "There's some kind of vapour out here..." They glanced over their shoulders apprehensively, where increasing amounts of wisps now floated. Celeste didn't want to leave them out there to be victimized, but she didn't want to risk letting the smokelike substance in with them, either.

Then, seeing that the men were backed into a corner, the mist struck, insinuating itself under their nostrils so it was drawn in with their next breath. A change seemed to come over them, and before her eyes they turned into ravening beasts, their human features distorted into vulturous parody with sharp pink skin and clawlike hands.

"No..." Celeste breathed in horror,

backing away.

"Open the door..." the one on the left, in a red captain's coat, snarled teasingly in an entirely different voice. He pulled out the pistol that hung at his belt, pointing it straight at her from behind the glass, the hard muzzle pressed right up against it.

Alarmed, Celeste cast around for a place to take cover; she doubted that even the thick double panes would stop a bullet from passing through. Then, through the archway behind her, she saw a swarm of the infected monsters beginning to pour in from the front of the house.

She stared with a sinking dread in her middle. She hadn't locked the front door.

She turned back to the deeper half of the room, and to her shock found that even the counsellor hadn't been spared; the contagion must already be spreading on the air the others had let in.

With no choice left to her, she whirled and fled down the stairs into the dark earthen cellar, hoping at least to escape their notice by hiding there, until she could think of some other way out.

Once she reached the bottom landing she slowed, looking around cautiously. The walls and ceiling were overgrown with gnarly roots and even thick green vines, hanging down like verdant stalactites. Beyond the dim circle of light from the mounted candle behind her, the shadowy basement faded into near blackness; she couldn't tell how long it went on for, but it seemed quiet and spacious.

In the hopes of finding a tunnel that led away from there, Celeste ventured deeper. She bent lower to clear the overhead curtain of branchlike growths, and wove between individual dangling stems.

She brushed against the leaves of a trailing ivy, and suddenly there was a soft white glow in the air around her, lighting the way. The draped roots lifted, parting to either side to show her a clear path ahead through the tangle. The plants nearby rustled though there were no drafts, almost as if whispering, "Princess...princess."

Celeste looked down at herself, and realized that the radiance was coming from her own dress, which was now a pristine white. Lifting her head, she regarded a drooping vine beside her, and raised her hand under it. It curled around to set itself gently on her palm, responding to her wordless beckon. And then she understood.

She was the White Princess.

And she knew what she had to do.

Turning back the way she had come, she hastened for the staircase through a lane of provided airspace that closed again behind her, as the shine of her gown gradually receded. As she went up the steps, a contingent of vines followed her through the air alongside, reaching and growing at the same speed as her travel.

At the top floor, Celeste sent her vines forward to touch the few affected individuals that had roamed into the vicinity. Upon contact, the leaves conveyed their healing, ridding them of the wisps' possession and returning the people to their original selves. Some of them buckled where they stood, as if drained of energy from the frenzy, or made unconscious by events they would rather forget.

**

The red princess shook her head to clear away the shadow darkening her vision. As awareness returned to her, she realized she was on her hands and knees. The last thing she remembered was being attacked by vulture-like creatures... She must have turned into one too. She lifted her head to look out the sitting room archway. What she saw was a blonde woman in a pure white gown, standing at the center of a mass of vines. They darted out in the direction of her every glance and gesture, wrapping themselves around each creature that came at her, restoring them to their human forms.

She can control the vines, Raianna thought, with dawning awe.

...Sister...

* * *

A crash sounded behind Celeste, and she glanced over her shoulder. Outside the back door, the creature in the red coat was striking his pistol against the window, fracturing the glass and dislodging shattered fragments. He'd already broken through the first pane. Once he'd made a hole big enough in the second, he reached his arm through and unlocked the door. As soon as he shoved it open, Celeste had her vines lash forth to meet him and his associate. The two stopped short in their charge, and their faces regained their identity. The man on the right slumped to the floor, out cold, but the captain only sagged, leaning hands on his knees.

Celeste redirected her attention to the last few of the afflicted who were still trying to get at her, and treated them too. Then she surveyed the room, but saw no more vulturous beasts. Several of the people were coming to, clambering to their feet with faint groans and sighs. Celeste let the vines withdraw back into the cellar.

She heard the click of a cocking gun.

She turned abruptly, but the captain had already aimed his pistol. The bullet he fired instantly pierced her near the heart, biting her with a sharp pang. She collapsed onto her back, and lay there in staring shock for a moment. She had never expected he would still wish her harm after he'd been cured. He leapt over her on his way past. Her eyelids grew heavy, and she could feel the darkness creeping in on her, the pain sapping her strength. Before long, her head lolled to the side, and the life went out of her.

***

The crack of a gunshot made Raianna whip around. Her stomach dropped with dread. She pushed her way through the interposing crowd, through the archway to the back room.

And there she came upon the body of her dead sister, shot through the chest, a spread of blood staining her pristine white gown. That was the one place the colour red should never appear. Grimly Raianna turned to see the man with the smoking gun flee out the front entrance, pursued by a mob of outraged subjects. The princess in crimson stormed out after him, eyes blazing.

He ran to the very edge of the jutting

grass-covered cliff, then turned back to the horde, which had stopped some distance back from the precipice. He pointed his pistol at them. He seemed to think that his escape was assured, as a shuttlecraft sluggishly rose through the clouds from below.

But then the ground under his feet gave way, the tip of the crag crumbling down toward a sheer miles-long drop, and he lost hold of his gun even as the red princess continued striding out from the throng toward him. At her command, the vines and roots in the remaining cliffside whipped out to catch him, lifting him up before her so she could stare at him face to face when she stopped just inches away – but then the bonds started tightening, coiling ever more constrictively around his limbs, his body...his neck.

From the crowd behind, the counsellor stepped closer to her. "Don't do it," he pleaded softly. But Raianna's gaze on the captain was merciless. He was going to pay for what he had done to her precious sister, so newly found, so senselessly lost.

***

The blood of the princess in white seeped through the ground of her home, down to the very heart of the Floating Land. There, the living consciousness recognized its beloved queen, recalled its primary instinct to protect her. The healing of the vines was redirected back through the earth to where Celeste lay crumpled, giving back what she had expended to the others of her people, but had not partaken of herself. Her gown began to glow again, clearing away the bloodstains, before fading.

Slowly, her eyes opened again to reveal pearl-grey irises, which reverted to their original green as she took a breath that set her heart to beating. Blinking, Celeste carefully stood up, and turned to survey the scene out the open front door. By the clifftop, her sister looked over her shoulder, and her vines' grip on the captain slackened as she saw with wonder that Celeste was alive.

The White Princess headed out to them, her steps measured and sure. The crowd parted for her, watching her with murmurs of amazement.

"...the Princess..."

"She lives!"

Celeste arrived beside her sister, gaze on the captain. "Set him down," she said calmly. "He knows not what he did."

Still staring at Celeste, Raianna had the vines unwind from around the captain's neck, then brought him back in so his feet touched the ground – but the roots stayed securely wrapped around his arms, to make sure he didn't try anything.

The man was panting through his ragged throat, his eyes wide on Celeste.

"You...I shot you..." he whispered hoarsely.

Celeste looked the captain square in the eye. "Take him and his accomplice to a correctional facility. Make sure they do enough selfless service to make up for what they've done."

"Yes, Princess," the counsellor agreed. He sent some men to gather the other criminal, and had a guard clamp cuffs on the captain's hands, so Raianna could withdraw the vines. Then the offenders were marched onto the very shuttle they'd been planning to commandeer as an escape.

The red princess turned to Celeste, extending both hands toward hers. "Sister," she breathed, and Celeste smiled at her, holding her hands and giving them a squeeze.

"Sorry I've been away so long. I never knew about any of this."

"I'm just grateful you're safe. But now that you're here, the people will wonder..."

Raianna murmured, looking around at the crowd.

"I know." Celeste's eyes were lowered. "I'll make the announcement. Have them gather in the throne room." It needed to be done – even though it meant she'd have to leave her foster mother behind. At least Farmer Ramsey would be satisfied that she'd found a home of her own. Maybe Celeste could even send some royal funds their way. After things were settled here, she would go back to the mainland to explain the situation to her family. She hoped they'd understand. Her people needed her here, to keep the island from falling apart.

As Raianna herded all the inhabitants of the island into the mansion, Celeste folded her hands, pensive gaze still on the ground. It all made sense – the story of how the White Princess had disappeared along with a long-distance shuttle, and her own history of how the Ramseys had found her abandoned in a remote field far in the southwest. The royal couple in the portrait had been her parents. She was sad she'd never known them, that she wouldn't get a chance to, now – sad that they were gone altogether. They looked like they had been good-hearted people.

The counsellor came back up to her from the island edge. "It's good to have you back, Princess," he said softly.

She met his eyes. "You knew my parents, before. Will you tell me more about them?"

He smiled. "I'd be honoured to." He set a hand on her shoulder as he headed past.

Drawing in a deep breath of crisp air, Celeste looked around at the island, and smiled. She didn't only consider it her duty to stay here. She loved this place. It was where she belonged.

Turning, Celeste proceeded inside,

head up and shoulders squared. She entered the Hall of the Rising Sun, where the few dozen native islanders and attendants of the royal family stood in a semicircle, watching Celeste with expectant hope. Raianna and the counsellor were foremost among them.

Pristine gown draping sedately on the floor behind her, Celeste stepped up onto the large circular marble dais, facing east with stature proud. "I am Celeste Silverborn, the White Princess and one true ruler of the Island in the Air. I have returned to my home, and protected it once already from the threat of harm. I have been brought back to life, to take my place as Preserver of Peace!" And the citizens cheered.

The End